For Ridley

First published 2020 by Nosy Crow Ltd
The Crow's Nest, 14 Baden Place
Crosby Row, London SE1 1YW
www.nosycrow.com

ISBN 978 1 78800 825 9

Nosy Crow and associated logos are trademarks and/or
registered trademarks of Nosy Crow Ltd.

A CIP catalogue record for this book is available from
the British Library.

Printed in China
Papers used by Nosy Crow are made from wood
grown in sustainable forests.

10 9 8 7 6 5 4 3

THERE'S A MOUSE IN MY HOUSE

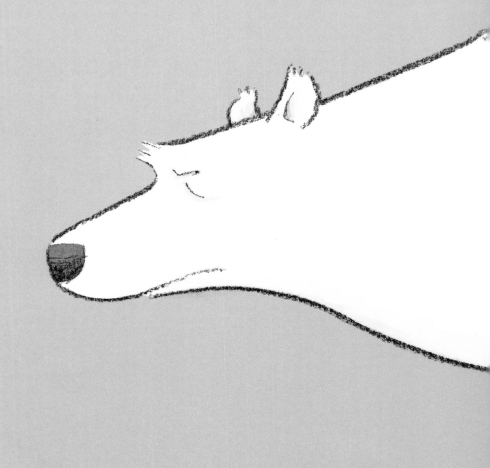

ROSS COLLINS

nosy crow

There's a mouse in my house.

How **he** got in, I'd like to know.
He's unpacked all his stuff just so.

That rodent can't live here,
oh no!
I'll tell him
that he has to go.

Would you believe it?
He said no!
I'll chuck him out
with one quick throw . . .

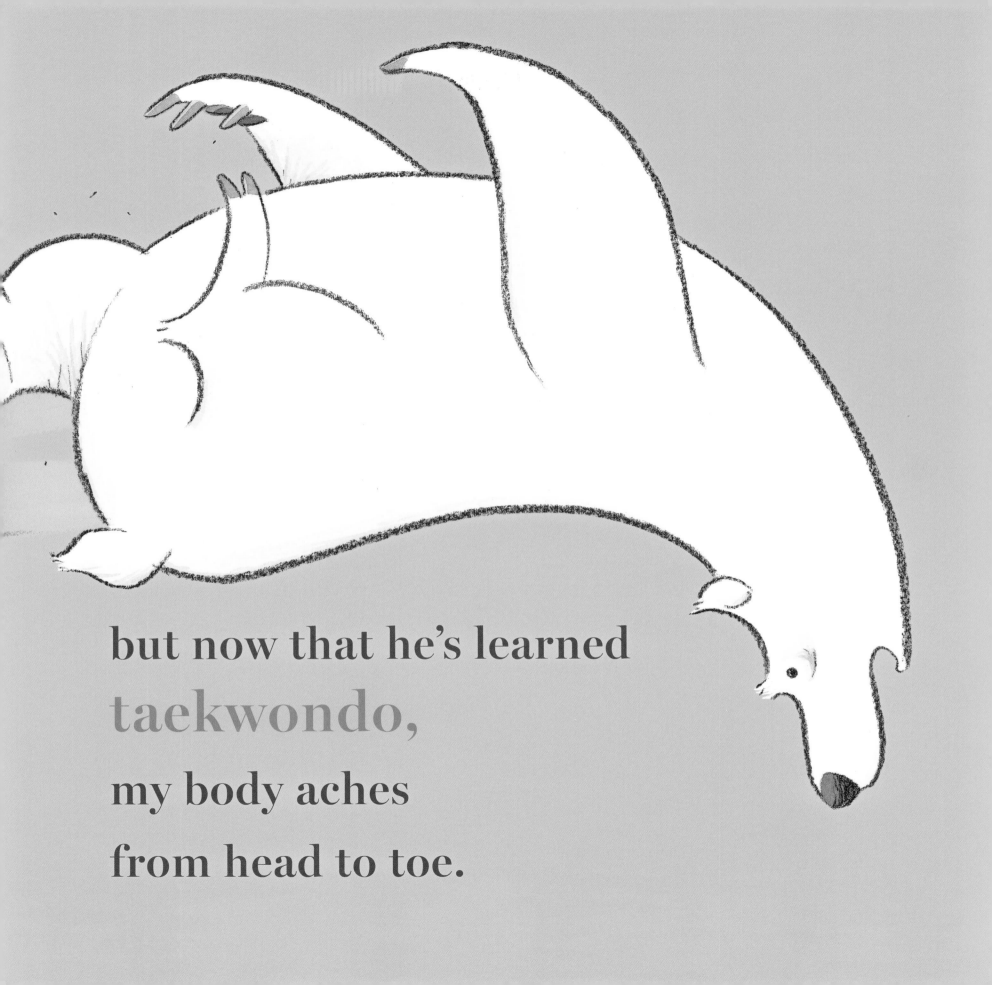

but now that he's learned
taekwondo,
my body aches
from head to toe.

There's lots of places he could go,
from Luxembourg or Mexico
to Timbuktu or Borneo,
but he just doesn't
want to know.

Our **taste** is not the same,
although
he wears nice boots
and fine chapeaux.
His cape is swell but even so . . .
why **won't** this mouse
say **cheerio?**

He may be **small** but even so
he eats just like a buffalo.
Just **where** he puts it,
I don't know.
He's left me
one pistachio.

At **night** he dances to and fro
to **soft rock** on his stereo.
He likes to put on
quite a show.

When will I sleep?
I do not know.

He's made my bathtub overflow!
It flooded the room down below,
so now I'm soaked from head to toe.

That's it!
I'm done!
He has to go!

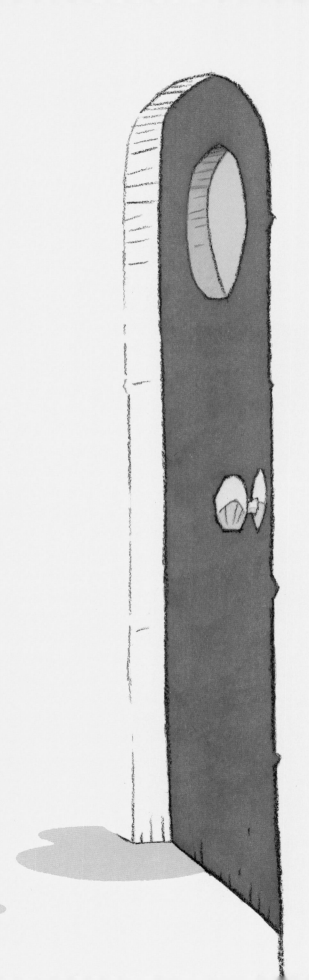

Knock!
Knock!

But **who** is **this**, I'd like to know?
Some folk are outside in the snow.
But **who'd** come here
to say hello?
Hang on –
don't open that!
Oh no!

Hey!

These mice
are nice!